BIRD ALPHABET

written by Llewellyn Teresa McKernan
illustrated by Heidi Petach

God made the birds,
so many there's one
for each alphabet letter.
Say them. It's fun!

Library of Congress Catalog Card Number 87-91986
©1988. The STANDARD PUBLISHING Company, Cincinnati, Ohio
Division of STANDEX INTERNATIONAL Corporation. Printed in U.S.A.

A is for the albatross.
Over seas it can go.

B is for a black bird.
This one's a crow.

C is for the chicken.
Corn is its snack.

D is for the duck
that goes "quack, quack."

E is for the eagle
with its big, wide wings.

F is for the flicker.
To tree trunks it clings.

G is for the goose
that makes a honking call.

H is for the hummingbird
that's so quick and small.

I is for the ibis
that builds a big nest.

J is for the blue jay
with its long, pointed crest.

K is for the kingfisher.
It loves to eat fish.

L is for the lark.
Seeds are its daily dish.

M is for the magpie,
walking with a strut!

N is for the nutcracker.
It loves to crack nuts.

O is for the owl
that cries "hoot, hoot."

P is for the pigeon
in its gray-feathered suit.

Q is for the quail
eating the wild berry.

R is for the robin
with its song so merry.

S is for the snipe
in little striped hoods.

T is for the turkey.
Wild ones live in woods.

U is for the upland sandpiper with its shoe-button eye.

V is for the vulture
that soars high in the sky.

W is for the wren.
It's lively, never dull.

X is for the xema
that we call a gull.

Y is for the yellowlegs.
In marshes its song is heard.

Z is for the zebra finch.
It's kept as a cage bird.

God made the birds,
each feather and wing.
They're in His care,
and His praises they sing.